SIT ON A POTATO PAN, OTIS!

MORE Palindromes
by JON AGEE

Farrar Straus Giroux
New York

For Bill and Jeanne Steig

PETITE "P"

LEE HAS A
RACECAR
AS A HEEL

DEOBOED

ED IS LOOPY POOLSIDE

NAIVE WAS I ERE I SAW EVIAN

NEPTUNE NUT PEN

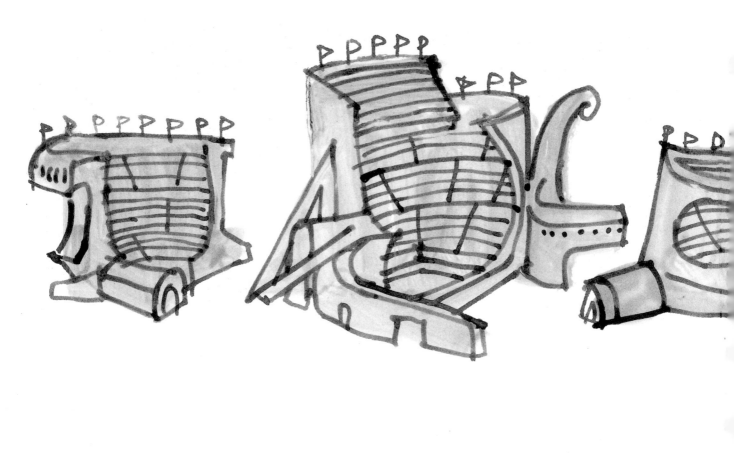

DESSERTS STRESS ED

PUMAS LIVEN EVIL SAM UP

DUMB MOBS BOMB MUD

BALD ELF
FLED LAB

POOCH COOP

SAGA SIGNING IS A GAS

KENNY TOLSTOY,
IN PERSON,
SIGNING HIS
LATEST SAGA

Acknowledgments

Most of the palindromes in this book grew (very slowly) out of my brain. The others were created, to the best of my knowledge, by the following people: John Baumann (DEOBOED); Andrea Cantrell (RED? NO WONDER from Michael Donner's *I Love Me, Vol. I*, Algonquin Books, Chapel Hill, North Carolina, 1996); Stephen J. Chism (DOG DOO? GOOD GOD! from his *From A to Zotamorf*, Word Ways Press, Morristown, New Jersey, 1992); Michael Donner (DRACULA VALU-CARD and SILOPOLIS, from his book mentioned above); Leigh Mercer (SIT ON A POTATO PAN, OTIS!, SOME MEN INTERPRET NINE MEMOS, and NO LEMONS, NO MELON!, from Howard W. Bergerson's *Palindromes and Anagrams*, Dover Press, New York, 1973); Mark Saltveit (NO PANIC, I NAP ON! and DESSERTS STRESS ED); and Béla Fleck's bass player, Victor Lemonte Wooten, via Jay Neale via Joanna Long (DO GEESE SEE GOD?). I found TONS OF UFOS! NOT! and DUMB MOBS BOMB MUD (originally from Web-site listings) in O. V. Michaelsen's *Words at Play* (Sterling Publishing Co., Inc., New York, 1998).

Coke, Evian, Honda, Pepsi, Stetson, and Tylenol are registered trademarks.

Library of Congress Cataloging-in-Publication Data
Agee, Jon.
Sit on a potato pan, Otis! : more palindromes / by Jon Agee. — 1st ed.
p.   cm.
ISBN 0-374-31808-5
1. Palindromes.   I. Title.
PN6371.Z44   1999
793.734—dc21   98-31783